Bravo, Chico Canta! Bravo!

Pat Mora & Libby Martinez

Pictures by

Amelia Lau Carling

Groundwood Books House of Anansi Press
Toronto Berkeley

Published in Canada and the USA in 2014 by Groundwood Books

Groundwood Books / House of Anansi Press
110 Spadina Avenue, Suite 801, Toronto, Ontario M5V 2K4
or c/o Publishers Group West
1700 Fourth Street, Berkeley, CA 94710

We acknowledge for their financial support of our publishing program the Government of Canada through the Canada Book Fund (CBF).

Library and Archives Canada Cataloguing in Publication
Mora, Pat, author
Bravo, Chico Canta! Bravo! / Pat Mora and Libby Martinez ; illustrated by Amelia Lau Carling.
Issued in print and electronic formats.
ISBN 978-1-55498-343-8 (bound).—ISBN 978-1-55498-345-2 (html)
1. Mice—Juvenile fiction. I. Martinez, Libby, author II. Carling, Amelia Lau, illustrator III. Title.
PZ7.M689Br 2014 j813'.54 C2013-905715-3
C2013-905716-1

The illustrations were done in watercolor and mixed media.
Design by Michael Solomon
Printed and bound in Malaysia

To my friend Patsy Aldana, respected publisher, editor and international literacy advocate. — PM

To Bill and Cissy, who love all creatures great and small, especially small. — LM

For Isabella Kai-lie and Nathan Koon-cho. — ALC

Chico Canta and his mouse family lived in an old theater. In their cozy home, they listened to orchestras play, to actors and actresses sing and to audiences clap. Sometimes the audience clapped for a long time, shouting, "Bravo! Bravo!" in Italian, which meant they liked the show.

"Hurry! Hurry! ¡Pronto! ¡Pronto!" sang Mrs. Canta. "Tonight, we're going to see the play *The Three Little Pigs*." She clapped her hands together and sang, "Let's form a line — una fila, por favor."

Mrs. Canta, who was round as a top, liked to sing and to speak many languages —English, Spanish and Italian. Mrs. Canta spoke to animals, too. She could speak Cricket, Spider and Moth.

Mrs. Canta loved to see her twelve children line up, tallest to smallest. “One, two, three, four, five, six, seven, eight, nine, ten, eleven…” said Mrs. Canta. “Where is Chico?”

“Not again!” sighed Chico’s eleven brothers and sisters.

Tiny Chico Canta was *never* where he should be — at the end of the line. Sometimes he was sleeping in his little bed. Sometimes he had crawled into the cookie jar. Sometimes he was hanging from the lampshade.

"Chiiiiiiicoooooo," sang Mrs. Canta as everyone scurried through the house, opening cabinets and looking behind curtains.

Chico was on top of the hat rack.

"Chico Canta!" said Mrs. Canta.

Chico climbed down and ran to the end of the line. All of his brothers and sisters frowned, and one of them pulled his tail.

Dressed in her prettiest dress, Mrs. Canta peeked out of their house to make sure that the kitten, Little Gato-Gato, was not close by. Little Gato-Gato, who lived in the theater, looked like a small orange tiger.

Quickly, the Canta family scurried up the stairs.

With their friends the crickets, spiders and moths, they watched the curtain rise, the lights twinkle and the musicians play. They laughed when the three little pigs built their houses out of straw, sticks and bricks. Chico pretended he was the big bad wolf and tried to blow his brothers and sisters over.

"Chico Canta!" whispered Mrs. Canta. She put her foot softly on his tail so he couldn't run around. Chico smiled, and then tried to blow her over.

When the play ended, the audience clapped a long time. The Canta family clapped, too.

"Bravo! Bravo!" everyone shouted.

With all of the clapping, the Cantas didn't hear Little Gato-Gato moving closer.

"Meow! Meow!" said Little Gato-Gato.

"Eeek! Eeek!" squeaked the Cantas.

"Hurry! Hurry! ¡Pronto! ¡Pronto!" said Mrs. Canta.

The Cantas ran as fast as they could. Little Gato-Gato was right behind them. Chico was ready to blow Little Gato-Gato over like the big bad wolf, but just in time, Mrs. Canta picked Chico up and carried him into their safe home.

That night, tucking each of their little ones into their beds, Mr. and Mrs. Canta softly sang, "Dulces sueños, sweet dreams."

Chico yawned and sang, "Dulces sueños, sweet dreams."

"Bilingual," said Mrs. Canta. "Bravo!"

The next morning, the Cantas began practicing. They liked to put on their own plays for their family and friends who lived in the theater.

Mr. Canta, a fine tailor and carpenter, whistled while he sewed costumes and built scenery for their new play, *The Three Little Pigs*. Mr. Canta sewed a wolf costume, three pig costumes, three flower costumes and four tree costumes. He also sewed one very tiny sun costume.

"Bow-wow," growled Chico. "I'm going to be the big bad wolf. Right, Mamá?"

"Wolves don't say 'Bow-wow,'" laughed one of Chico's brothers. "Dogs say 'Bow-wow.'" His other brothers and sisters giggled.

"How smart you are, Chico," said Mrs. Canta. "You can speak Spanish, Italian and Dog, too. Little Gato-Gato would be scared of you if you growled, 'Bow-wow.'"

Chico's brothers and sisters giggled again.

"We have a special part for you to play," said Mr. Canta.

"I love special parts!" said Chico.

"We know you do," said Mrs. Canta.

Mr. Canta showed Chico the post he had made so Chico could be the tallest mouse in the play. Chico put on his sun costume and climbed to the top. Chico's brothers and sisters looked up at him and smiled. Chico beamed!

Every day the Cantas practiced *The Three Little Pigs*. Mrs. Canta directed their animal friends. She whispered, “Chirp-chirp,” to the crickets who played the music. She whispered, “Pss-pss,” to the spiders who raised the curtain and moved the lights. She whispered, “Whh-whh,” to the moths who practiced leading the audience to their seats.

Chico liked to help Mrs. Canta direct. He whispered, “Chirp-chirp, pss-pss, whh-whh.”

“Bilingual,” said Mr. Canta. “Bravo!”

Finally, it was time for the Canta family's special night. They invited all their relatives who lived in the theater to see their play — grandmothers and grandfathers, aunts and uncles, first cousins and second cousins, third cousins and fourth cousins. They did not invite Little Gato-Gato.

Mrs. Canta whispered, "Zzz-zzz," to the fireflies to turn on the flashing sign. She whispered, "Whh-whh," to the moths to take everyone to their seats. She whispered, "Chirp-chirp," to the crickets to start playing the music. She whispered, "Pss-pss," to the spiders to get ready to raise the curtain on the small stage.

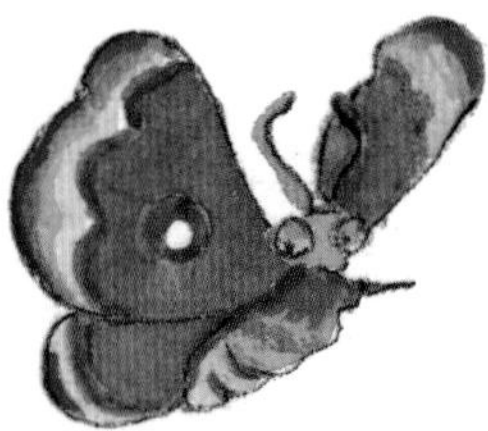

"Let's form a line — una fila, por favor," sang Mrs. Canta.

"I have one big bad wolf, three little pigs, three flowers, four trees and…" Mrs. Canta said. "Where is my sun? Where is Chico?"

"Not again!" sighed Chico's brothers and sisters.

Mr. Canta found Chico smiling at himself in the mirror.

When the curtain went up, Chico Canta waved at everyone from his perch. He bowed and said, "Buenas noches, good evening!" He raised his hands and directed the audience, who answered, "Buenas noches, good evening!"

"Bilingual," said Chico Canta. "Bravo!"

The play started, and the audience laughed and laughed when the little pigs built their houses out of straw, sticks and bricks.

On his perch, Chico began to look around. He looked up and down. He looked to the right and to the left.

All of a sudden, in the shadows on the other side of a low wall, Chico saw something move. While everyone was laughing at the big bad wolf, Chico saw something coming closer — and closer.

"Eeek! Little Gato-Gato!" yelled Chico, pointing at the shadows. "Bow-wow!" growled Chico in his loudest voice.

Then he quickly directed the audience, who growled, "Bow-wow! Bow-wow! Bow-wow!"

Little Gato-Gato jumped and ran away as fast as he could.

Everyone clapped for a long time. Chico bowed and bowed.

"Bilingual!" everyone cheered. "Bravo, Chico Canta! Bravo!"

Author's Note

Life regularly offers us new challenges and new pleasures. One of my new pleasures is writing books for children with my daughter Libby Martinez. Libby is a lawyer and an excellent writer. We both love reading and books, and now we're discovering that we have great fun writing together.

I'd read the kernel of this bilingual joke years ago in a book of Mexican American folktales. The idea seemed one children would enjoy, and so I'm grateful to my friend Patsy Aldana, the former publisher of Groundwood Books, for her interest in sharing this story and for again teaming me (now us) up with Amelia Lau Carling's wonderful talent.

Years ago, in a Cincinnati library, I was explaining the word *bilingual* to a group of students. I asked, "What would I be if I could speak three languages?" and a clever student enthusiastically responded, "Very bilingual!" The word *multilingual* seemed too cumbersome for this story, so Libby and I decided that "Bilingual! Bravo!" allowed us to move the story along. We know that astute parents, teachers and librarians will introduce the multisyllabic *multilingual* when appropriate.

Bravo, Libby, for wisely deciding to join the world of children's books as an author! Lucky me.

Pat Mora